To my dad

"NO!"
said Rabbit

Marjoke
Henrichs

Published by
PEACHTREE PUBLISHING COMPANY INC.
1700 Chattahoochee Avenue
Atlanta, Georgia 30318-2112
www.peachtree-online.com

Text and illustrations © 2021 by Marjoke Henrichs

First published in Great Britain in 2021
by Scallywag Press Ltd
10 Sutherland Row, London SW1V 4JT
First United States version published in 2021
by Peachtree Publishing Company Inc.

The illustrations were created with wooden stick,
ink, gouache, and colored pencil.

Printed in October 2020 in China
10 9 8 7 6 5 4 3 2 1
First Edition
ISBN: 978-1-68263-294-9

Cataloging-in-Publication Data is available
from the Library of Congress

PEACHTREE
ATLANTA

"Time to get dressed," said Mom.

"NO!"

said Rabbit.

But that is my favorite top and my pants with the big pockets . . .

First, Rabbit put his pants on . . .

inside out,

upside down,

sideways,

and the right way 'round!

And then his top . . .

inside out,

upside down,

sideways,

and the right way 'round!

"Time for breakfast!" said Mom.

"NO!"

said Rabbit.

But I **can** see juicy
orange carrots . . .

Rabbit ate one carrot.
Then another
and another.

Then a little one
and a big one . . .

And a few more until . . .

. . . they were all gone!

And *then* he had a
cookie or two when
Mom wasn't looking!

"Time to go outside," said Mom.

"NO!"
said Rabbit.

But those **are** my lovely rain boots . . .

Rabbit put his boots on and went outside.

He jumped in the puddles

and sat in one too!

He cycled,

watered the radishes,

then scored
a goal!

He played
with his kite

and then
his stilts.

"Time for a drink," said Mom.

"NO!" said Rabbit. "I am not thirsty."

"Time for a snack, then," said Mom.

"NO!" said Rabbit. "I am not hungry."

"Time for your potty," said Mom.

"NO!" said Rabbit. "I am too big for the potty."

"Time to go inside now," said Mom.

"NO!" said Rabbit. "I want to stay outside."

"Time for a bath now," said Mom.

"NO NO NO NO NO NO!"

"I don't need a bath!"

"But your bath is lovely and warm!" said Mom. "I am waiting . . ."

"NO!"

said Rabbit.

"I am hiding."

"I found you!" said Mom.
"Come with me."

"NO!"

said Rabbit.

But there **are** lots and lots of bubbles **and** my Ducky too . . .

"Time to get out
of the bath now!"
said Mom.

"NO!"
said Rabbit.
"I don't want to get out!"
Splosh! Splish!
Splash!

"But it's time for cuddles!" said Mom.

"Yes!"

said Rabbit.

"I LOVE cuddles."

"Now, off to bed little Rabbit," said Mom.

"NO, no, no, no . . ."

Z Z Z Z Z Z Z Z